What a Mess, Fang Fang!

Written and illustrated by Sally Rippin

An easy-to-read SOLO
for beginning readers

SOLOS

Southwood Books Limited
3 – 5 Islington High Street
London N1 9LQ

First published in Australia by Omnibus Books 1998

Published in the UK under licence from
Omnibus Books by
Southwood Books Limited, 2000.

This edition produced for The Book People Ltd.,
Hall Wood Avenue, Haydock, St Helens WAII 9UL

Reprinted 2003

Text and illustrations copyright © Sally Rippen 1998
Cover design by Lyn Mitchell

ISBN 1 903207 15 0

Printed in China

A CIP catalogue record for this book is available
from the British Library

For Gabriel when he's six

Chapter 1

Fang Fang did not like her twin cousins, Ling May and Ling Sun. If Fang Fang ate wontons and her cousins ate wontons, it was always Fang Fang who dropped soy sauce on her top.

"What a mess, Fang Fang!" her mother would say. "Why can't you be clean like your cousins?"

Ling May and Ling Sun were better at everything than Fang Fang was.

They were better at playing the piano.

They were better at school work.

They even used chopsticks better
than Fang Fang did.

This made Fang Fang cross.

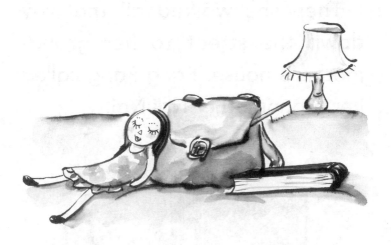

Chapter 2

One day Fang Fang was so cross that she wanted to run away from home.

She put some things in a bag: her doll, her toothbrush, and the book she liked best.

Then she walked all the way down the street to her grand-mother's house. Fang Fang called her grandmother Nai Nai.

Fang Fang's grandmother opened the door. She had been cooking, and there was flour on her hands. She could see that Fang Fang was cross.

"Fang Fang," she said, "do you want to stay with me and eat some home-made wontons?"

"Oh yes, Nai Nai!" said Fang Fang.

So Fang Fang's grandmother rang Fang Fang's mother and father to tell them that Fang Fang was staying with her.

Chapter 3

Fang Fang and her grandmother sat down at the table to eat wontons. The wontons were very slippery. The chopsticks were very thin.

Fang Fang picked up one wonton with her chopsticks and popped it in her mouth. Then she picked up another one and popped it in her mouth.

Then Fang Fang picked up a third wonton, but ... oh dear! ... there was soy sauce on her top again!

She began to cry.

"Do not cry, Fang Fang!" said her grandmother. "We can wash your top. Eat some more wontons. I will get you another top."

While her grandmother left to look for a clean top, Fang Fang ate up all the wontons.

With her fingers!

"Good! Good!" Fang Fang's grandmother said when she came back with a clean top for Fang Fang. "I am happy that you like my wontons. I will make you some more."

Fang Fang gave her grand-
mother a big hug. She loved her
Nai Nai.

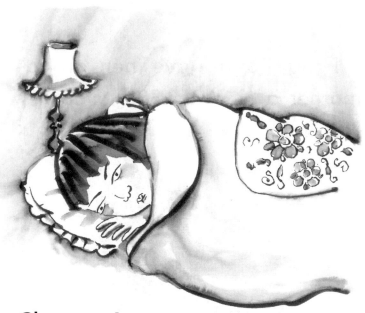

Chapter 4

After dinner it was time for bed. Fang Fang put on her grandmother's top and snuggled down under the sheets. But she could not sleep! She rolled this way and that way, but something stuck into her.

What *could* it be?

Fang Fang put her hand in the pocket of her grandmother's top. Inside was something hard and cool.

She took it out. It was a small green stone, cut into the shape of a cat. There was a hole at the top for a piece of string. It was very pretty.

Fang Fang held the small cat up to the lamp. She could see her fingers through it.

She put it on her lips. The green stone cat felt cool.

Fang Fang wanted to keep the cat. If she had a cat made from green stone she would have something special to show her cousins.

When Fang Fang woke up next morning, her grandmother was still asleep.

Fang Fang took off her grandmother's top and put on her own top, which had been washed and dried.

She put the green stone cat in her pocket and walked home.

Chapter 5

At school Fang Fang saw Ling May and Ling Sun. "Hi, Fang Fang!" they said.

Fang Fang put her hand in her pocket. She felt the smooth stone cat, but did not take it out.

The twins walked past.

Rick walked up to her. Fang Fang liked Rick.

"Look, Fang Fang!" Rick said. In his hands was a small lizard.

Fang Fang smiled. She put her hand in her pocket again. The green stone cat was still there, but once again she did not take it out.

The school bell rang.

Chapter 6

In class, Fang Fang's teacher said, "Does anyone have something to show us today?"

Fang Fang put up her hand.

"Yes, Fang Fang?"

"Um ... nothing," Fang Fang said.

Ling May and Ling Sun giggled.

Fang Fang put her hand down quickly. The green stone cat made a small bump in her pocket.

After school Fang Fang ran all the way to her grandmother's house.

Her grandmother was busy
making wontons. The back door
was open, and Fang Fang crept in.

Fang Fang went into the bedroom. Grandmother's top was still hanging on the door.

Fang Fang put the green stone cat back into the pocket and ran home.

Chapter 7

That night Fang Fang and her mother and father came to Grandmother's house to have wontons for dinner. Her cousins and their parents came too.

Grandmother put a very big wonton in Fang Fang's bowl.

"That wonton is so big you cannot drop it!" she said.

Ling May and Ling Sun giggled.

Fang Fang stuck her chopstick into the big wonton. She picked it up and bit into it.

"Ow!" she said. "There is something hard in my wonton!"

"Oh?" said Fang Fang's mother.
"Something hard and cool!" said Fang Fang.

"Oh?" said Fang Fang's father.

Fang Fang dropped the wonton back into her bowl.

"Something hard and cool and *green*!" said Fang Fang.

"Oh?" said Fang Fang's grand-mother.

What *could* it be?

Inside Fang Fang's wonton was the green stone cat!

"How did that get there?" asked Fang Fang's grandmother, smiling. "That cat is made from *jade*. Jade is very special. To find a green jade cat in your wonton is lucky. It's like magic! It looks as if you will have to keep it!"

Chapter 8

Fang Fang picked up the small cat made of jade. It felt cool. She was very happy. She felt very special.

"Thank you, Nai Nai," said Fang Fang softly.

Fang Fang's grandmother winked
at Fang Fang.

Fang Fang showed the jade cat
to her twin cousins.

"What is it?" asked Ling May.
"I want one too!" wailed Ling
Sun.

Fang Fang's cousins made a big mess opening up all the wontons. They were looking for green jade cats. They *both* got soy sauce on their tops!

Their mother was very cross with them. "What a mess!" she said. "Why can't you be clean like Fang Fang?"

And do you know what?
Fang Fang did not spill any!

Sally Rippin

When I was six, my best friend had a book about flower fairies. I loved that book. I wanted to have it for myself, so I could look at the pictures every day.

One day, when I was playing at my friend's house, I put the book in my bag and took it home.

When I saw my friend at school the next day, I felt very bad. I showed her the book and told her I was sorry I had taken it. She said it didn't matter. Then, on Christmas Day, do you know what my friend gave me? A flower fairies book. A new one. With my name in it!

The Story of Fang Fang

There is a real Fang Fang, and Sally Rippin has written and illustrated two other books about her, *Speak Chinese, Fang Fang!* and *Fang Fang's Chinese New Year.*

Sally was born in Australia, but grew up living mostly in Asian countries. This made her feel different from other children. Then she met Fang Fang, who became her friend. Fang Fang felt different too. Like Sally, she was not living in her own country.

When Sally lived in China, she learned how to paint in the Chinese way. Her pictures of Fang Fang are a funny mix of Chinese and Australian ways of painting.

More Solos!

Dog Star
Janeen Brian and Ann James

The Best Pet
Penny Matthews and Beth Norling

Fuzz the Famous Fly
Emily Rodda and Tom Jellett

Cat Chocolate
Kate Darling and Mitch Kane

Jade McKade
Jane Carroll and Virginia Barrett

I Want Earrings
Dyan Blacklock and Craig Smith

What a Mess Fang Fang
Sally Rippin

Cocky Colin
Richard Tulloch and Stephen Axelsen